# The Cup FinaL

## Other titles in the same series

### Ghost Goalie
The Tigers football team are full of confidence about the next match. But their coach falls ill just before they are due to play! The Tigers are desperate. How can they win without him? Perhaps they can, with a very special bit of ghostly help . . .

### Save the Pitch
It's the crucial last game of the season and the Tigers football team must win to go to the top of the League. But the pitch has been invaded by workmen laying new pipes, and it looks like the game will be called off. Can the Tigers get help – fast?

### The Terrible Trainer
The Tigers football team have a substitute coach, but he is mean and shouts a lot. He makes the Tigers feel awful. How can they get rid of Mr Bawl and find a coach who will make sure they can win?

### Tigers on Television
The Tigers football team have a nail-biting match to play, and a local TV crew has come to film them in action. But the TV cameras have a terrible effect on the team's ghost trainer and he can't coach them properly! What can the Tigers do?

### Ghost Striker
The Tigers football team are facing a difficult away match against a tough team, but they have got the special help of their ghost goalie . . . or have they? Things look bad when an old opponent arrives – intent on revenge!

# The Cup Final

## J. BURCHETT AND S. VOGLER

### Illustrated by Guy Parker-Rees

**BLOOMSBURY**

LONDON  BERLIN  NEW YORK

*For Simon and Robin Middleburgh*

Bloomsbury Publishing, London, Berlin and New York

First published in Great Britain in 1998 by Bloomsbury Publishing Plc
36 Soho Square, London, W1D 3QY
This edition published in July 2010

A CIP catalogue record of this book is available from the British Library

ISBN 978 1 4088 0830 6

FSC
**Mixed Sources**
Product group from well-managed
forests and other controlled sources

Cert no. SGS-COC-2061
www.fsc.org
© 1996 Forest Stewardship Council

Printed in Great Britain by Clays Ltd, St Ives plc, Bungay, Suffolk

1 3 5 7 9 10 8 6 4 2

www.bloomsbury.com/childrens

THE TIGERS

Mona (GK)

Terry  RICK  LISA  Blocker

Joe  ROB  Ellen  Kim

Bullseye  Billy Bright

Logo  Coach Mr. Bright

# The Cup Final

Billy Bright and the Tigers
Football Team were in the final
of the UEFA Cup. If they won,
they would go into the record
books. The Under-Elevens
Football Association Cup had

never been won by nine-year-olds before.

The Tigers were on the Tottingham Town pitch. They were supposed to be warming-up but they weren't. They were standing round their coach, Billy's dad. Mr Bright had been reaching for a ball that had

gone over. His head was stuck
in the railings. Billy and Rob
pulled at Dad's trousers. He
didn't budge.

'Ouch!' he yelled. 'Mind my
ears.'

'Try wriggling your head, Mr
Bright,' said Ellen.

'It hurts,' groaned Billy's
dad.

'Bend the railings, Mr Bright,' suggested Bullseye.

'I'm not Superman,' moaned Mr Bright. 'This is a job for . . . the fire brigade.'

'Your mum's a fire officer, Blocker,' said Lisa. 'Is she on duty?'

'Yes,' said Blocker. 'I'll phone her. She'll be really

pleased. She thought she was going to miss the match.'

Blocker went to find a telephone.

'But how am I going to coach you?' said Mr Bright.

His bottom was facing the pitch.

'The fire brigade will get you free soon,' said Billy.

'Billy'll coach us till then, Mr Bright,' said Kim.

'He's a good coach,' said Terry.

'When he gets going!' added Bullseye.

'Still got your book, Billy?' asked Mona the goalkeeper.

Whenever Billy's dad couldn't coach, Billy stepped in. The Tigers thought Billy and his coaching book were really good. They didn't know Billy's secret. Billy didn't have a book. He was helped by Springer Spannell – Tottingham Town's most famous goalkeeper. Everyone had heard of Springer but only Billy could see him. Springer Spannell was . . . a

ghost! Billy wasn't allowed to tell anyone. It was in Springer's PhIFA rules.

The Tigers ran on to the pitch. The opposition had already arrived. They looked very big. Billy looked round for Springer. Springer always turned up when he was needed. But there was no sign of him yet.

'What's first?' asked Joe.

'Ummm,' said Billy.

He was a terrible coach on his own. He remembered something he'd heard on the telly.

'Squat thrusts, arm stretches, side bends,' he called. '. . . Or was it arm thrusts, side stretches and squat bends?'

Rob tried a couple of side thrusts and fell over. Lisa flung

both arms out at once and
knocked Ellen and Bullseye
flying. Terry did a squatting
arm bend. It hit Blocker on the
nose just as he arrived back
from the phone.

'That's a funny way to warm
up,' said a voice.

Billy turned. There was a

16

man sitting in the Mayor's seat.
He was wobbly round the
edges. Billy could see right
through him. It was like
looking through a banana jelly.

'Springer!' yelled Billy.

'Spring?' asked Blocker.

'Okay, Coach,' said Ellen.

The Tigers started springing

17

round the pitch. Rob sprang off to the toilet.

'Sorry I'm late, Billy,' said Springer. 'I had to iron my kit. Where's your dad this time?'

'Over there,' mumbled Billy, embarrassed. 'He's stuck.'

'Oh dear,' said Springer. 'Tell him to rub butter on his ears. Now let's get started. Who are you playing?'

'Nutfield Road,' said Billy.

'The Nutters!' gasped Springer. 'We'll have to keep an eye on them.'

'Why?'

'I've seen them play, lad,' said Springer. 'They're a nasty side. They're always up to something.'

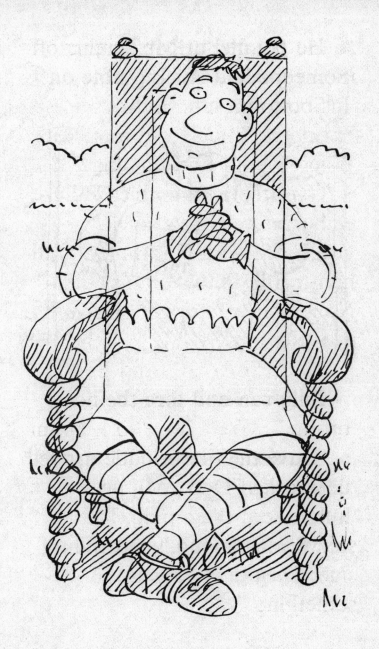

He pointed at Mr Bright.
Someone had stuck a note on
his bottom.

Billy ran and tore the note
off.

'Have the fire brigade arrived
yet?' asked Dad. 'My neck
hurts.'

'Won't be long,' said Billy.

\*

The crowd started waving their scarves. The Mayor took his seat. The UEFA cup stood gleaming in front of him. The referee called the teams over. Close up, the Nutters looked even bigger. They wore a dirty

grey and black kit. The Tigers suddenly felt very small.

'The Nutters don't play fair,' said Springer. 'Tell the team to watch out for dirty tricks.'

Billy told the Tigers in a whisper. He didn't want the Nutters to hear. The teams got into position. The referee tossed a coin. The Tigers won. They chose the town hall end.

It would be the Nutters' kick-off.

'Where's Rob?' shouted Blocker.

The Tigers looked round anxiously.

'Let's get on with it,' growled the Nutters' captain. 'If he's not here – tough!'

'Well . . .' said the referee.

Even *he* looked scared of the Nutters.

'I'll go and find him,' said Billy.

But as he ran to look, the match started. There were only nine Tigers on the pitch!

Billy started searching round.

'Have you seen Rob anywhere?' he asked Dad.

'All I can see is this ants' nest,' said Dad, gloomily. 'Have the fire brigade arrived yet? My back hurts.'

'Won't be long,' said Billy.

Then he heard a shout.

'Help! I'm stuck in the toilet!'

Billy ran and unlocked the toilet door. Rob tumbled out.

'The Nutters shut me in,' he wailed.

'Quick!' said Billy. 'The match has started.'

And, at that moment, they heard the roar of the crowd. Someone had scored. Billy and

Rob raced back on to the field.

'Where've you been?'
demanded Ellen.

'We're one-nil down,' said
Rick.

'We're going to lose!'
groaned Bullseye.

'No we're not,' said Billy.
'We're all here now.'

But then Billy realised he
couldn't see Springer. He had

no time to find him. It was the
Tigers' kick-off. Billy passed to
Kim but she was knocked
flying by a late challenge. The
Nutters had possession. They
headed for the goal. They
looked mean and hard. The

Tigers' defence wanted to run away. Billy knew he should be shouting instructions. He needed Springer's help and he needed it now.

And then Billy saw Springer. Springer was standing on the Mayor's head.

'What are you doing?' shouted Billy.

'Shaking with fright,' wailed Blocker.

'Not you, Blocker,' sighed Billy.

'Looking for Rob,' called Springer.

'Rob's here!' shouted Billy.

'Wish I wasn't,' said Rob.

Springer suddenly pointed at the Tigers' goal.

'What's the matter with Mona?' he shouted.

Mona seemed to be dancing in the goal-mouth. She was twitching and jerking. She didn't notice the Nutters coming towards her. She didn't see the

ball hit the back of the net. The
Nutters were two-nil up. But
Mona just kept jigging about.

'Goalkeeping wasn't like that
in my day,' said Springer,
climbing down the Mayor.

'What's the matter, Mona?'
shouted Billy.

'It's my hands,' sobbed
Mona. 'They're itching. They're
driving me mad!'

'They've used itching
powder,' said Springer crossly.

'Better get those gloves off
her.'

Billy took Mona off the
pitch.

'What are we going to do
without Mona?' Billy asked
Springer.

'Don't ask me,' said Terry.

'You're the coach,' said Lisa.

'Someone's got to go in goal,' said Springer.

'Someone's got to go in goal,' said Billy.

'Not me!' shouted the other

nine Tigers together.

'Looks like it's you, lad,' said Springer.

'I can't go in goal!' wailed Billy.

'Yes you can!' shouted the other nine Tigers together.

Billy stood in the goalmouth. He could feel his knees

chattering teeth →

knocking together. Springer stood by the post.

'It's no good,' hissed Billy. 'I'm not a goalkeeper.'

The Nutters heard him. They laughed.

'Don't worry,' said Springer. 'I'll coach you.'

'I wish you'd play instead of me,' said Billy.

'Sorry lad,' said Springer, shaking his head. 'PhIFA rule number thirteen. *A ghost coach – that's me – cannot come on as a substitute. If he does he gets the sack –* I disappear.'

There was nothing for it. Billy couldn't let the team down.

'Remember, lad,' said

Springer. 'Goalkeepers are not there just to stop shots. You've got to be ready to launch a counter-attack.'

'I'll be lucky to touch the ball,' wailed Billy.

'Listen to me,' said Springer firmly. 'Keep on your toes, ready to move. Don't take your

eyes off the ball. You can do it, lad.'

The play was coming Billy's way. He could hear the Nutters jeering at him.

'Ignore them,' said Springer. 'Watch out for that striker. Tell Blocker to tackle.'

'Tackle him, Blocker!'

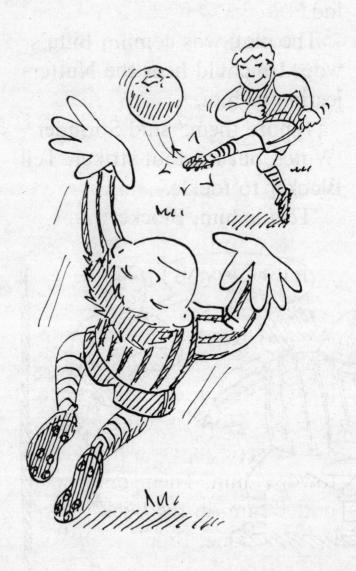

shouted Billy desperately. 'Er
. . . Lisa? . . . Rick? . . . Terry?
. . . Someone!'

But the Tigers' defenders
were cowering. The Nutters
broke through easily.

'It's up to you, lad,' said
Springer. 'Stop shaking.
Narrow the angle . . . that's it
. . . he's got it on the left foot
. . . dive to your right!'

Billy closed his eyes and
dived. There was a roar from
the crowd. The Nutters must
have scored again. Billy opened
his eyes. He wished he hadn't.
There were boots rushing
towards him. Then someone
patted him on the back.

'Well done, Billy!'

'You're a star!'
'Good work, lad.'
Billy realised he was clutching the ball! Somehow he had saved the goal.

Billy got ready to kick the ball. The Nutters weren't in a hurry to get back up the field.

'He was lucky,' snarled the striker.

'He won't kick it far,' said a defender.

'He's too weedy!' shouted the goalkeeper.

'We'll boot it straight back in the net,' sneered the Nutters' captain.

'Lean into it,' Springer told

Billy. 'Take your foot as far back as you can. That'll give it power. Watch the ball all the time. Off you go.'

Billy kicked the ball with all his might. It sailed over the heads

of the Tigers. It sailed over the
heads of the Nutters. It sailed
straight towards the Nutters'
goal. The Nutters' goalie had
come forwards to jeer at Billy.
The ball sailed over his head,
bounced four times and came to

45

rest just over the goal-line. Billy had scored from a goalkeeper's punt! It was two-one. The Tigers were in with a chance.

The whistle blew for half-time. Billy's dad was still stuck. But the fire brigade had arrived at last.

Billy and the Tigers huddled round. They knew the Nutters would want their revenge in the second half. And they weren't looking forward to it. The Tigers bit nervously into their half-time oranges. Springer began his team talk. But Billy wasn't listening. He had begun to sneeze and he couldn't stop.

'Bless you!' said Springer.

Then Blocker sneezed. And

Lisa. And Joe. And soon all the Tigers were sneezing their heads off.

'I think . . . a-tishoo . . . we've all got a cold,' sniffed Bullseye.

'I think we're allergic to the Nutters!' wheezed Rick.

'I think there's something wrong with . . . atchoo . . . these oranges!' gasped Kim.

'Quick!' shouted Springer.
'Throw them away. The Nutters
have put . . . wa-a-choo
. . . pepper on them!'

'Throw them away!'
spluttered Billy. 'The Nutters
have put . . . wa-a-choo . . .
pepper on them!'

The Nutters hadn't waited for the second half to get their revenge.

'Let's tell the referee,' sniffed Ellen.

'We can't prove anything,' said Rick.

The Tigers shuffled on to the pitch. Mona ran up. She was ready to go back in goal.

'I missed my half-time orange,' she complained.

'You were lucky,' snuffled Blocker.

It was the Tigers' kick off but their eyes were streaming. Bullseye thought he was passing to Billy but the ball went straight to the Nutters'

captain. She began a forwards
run. Lisa ran up to challenge.
She missed completely and
collided with Terry. Blocker
could see someone charging

towards him. He did a brilliant
sliding tackle. Well, it would
have been a brilliant sliding
tackle . . . if it hadn't been on
the referee!

'Sorry, Ref,' he quavered.

He waited to be sent off. But the referee had other things on his mind. There was a pile-up in the Tigers' goalmouth. At the bottom of the heap was the Nutters' captain.

'What's going on?' shouted the referee.

The referee blew his whistle. The Tigers blew their noses. The referee pointed to the penalty spot. The Nutters' captain placed the ball on the penalty spot.

'Tell Mona to sway to the right but dive to the left,' shouted Springer.'

Billy whispered to Mona. The players cleared the penalty area. Mona crouched ready. The crowd was silent. The Nutters' captain ran at the ball. She saw Mona sway to the right. So she hammered the ball

towards the left-hand corner of
the net. The Nutters started
cheering. It had to be a goal.

*

But Mona was ready. She made
a tremendous dive
to the left.

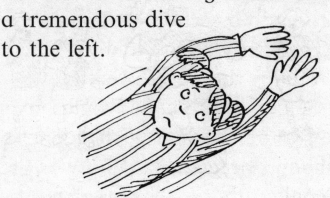

She hit the ground, the ball safe
in her hands. The Tigers
cheered. Springer swung on the
goalpost in excitement.

'What a save!' yelled the
crowd.

'That was just like Springer
Spannell!' yelled Lisa's
grandad.

'Ti-gers!' yelled the fire
brigade.

\*

The fire officers had managed to undo a section of the fence. They turned Dad and his railings round so he could see the action. Well, he would have seen the action if his head hadn't been stuck. As it was, he could only see the corner flag.

'Don't you worry, Mr
Bright,' said Blocker's mum,
picking up the crowbar. 'We'll
have you out in a jiffy. Wait a
minute . . . my boy's got the
ball. Did you see that? What a
pass! Now it's Joe . . . on to
Bullseye. To Kim . . . and over
to Billy. Mind that defender . . .
it's okay, he's feinted round her.

He's coming up to the goal!
Can he do it?'

The crowd roared.

'What's going on?' wailed
Dad.

'Billy's scored!' shrieked
Blocker's mum, waving her
crowbar.

'Two-all!' yelled the fire
brigade.

'Good play,' said Springer.
'You've shown them. You don't
have to cheat to win.'

'We haven't won yet,' panted
Billy.

'Get back out there then,'
said Springer. 'Go for your hat-
trick.'

The Nutters were looking tired.
They were a mean, hard side
but they weren't fit. The Tigers

60

soon got possession. Rick
passed to Lisa who flicked the
ball on to Terry. Blocker took
it from him and ran up the
wing. Then it was Joe. He
back-heeled it to Kim. She
pushed it forwards to Rob who
lobbed it over to Ellen. She
found Bullseye. The Nutters ran
backwards and forwards but

they couldn't keep up. Billy had
plenty of space. Bullseye
chipped the ball to him. Then
the Nutters' captain came
lumbering over. She had an
ugly look on her face. She leapt
at Billy in a high, vicious
tackle. But at the last minute,
Billy swerved. The Nutters'

captain flew past him and thumped heavily on to the pitch.

Now it was just Billy and the goalkeeper. Billy knew he had to score. Time was running out. He dribbled to the right, swayed to the left and watched the goalie dive. Then he punted the ball right into the centre of the net.

The final whistle blew. Billy Bright had got his hat-trick. And the Tigers had won the UEFA Cup.